When he arrived in Rabbit Town
it was chock-a-block with traffic,
Buses and cars roared past
on either side of him.
Everyone seemed to be in such a hurry.
He thought they must all have
very important things to do.
The main street frightened him.

Suddenly the traffic stopped with a screech of brakes.
Mr. Bear did not understand about the red traffic lights.
He felt sure something had gone wrong.
Perhaps, he thought, the engines had got stuck

because they had worked so hard.
Perhaps a helpful push
would put everything right.
He pushed. You can see what happened.

Then he found a quiet house
whose door stood wide open.
He knocked and took off his hat
ready to bow politely,
but there was nobody inside.

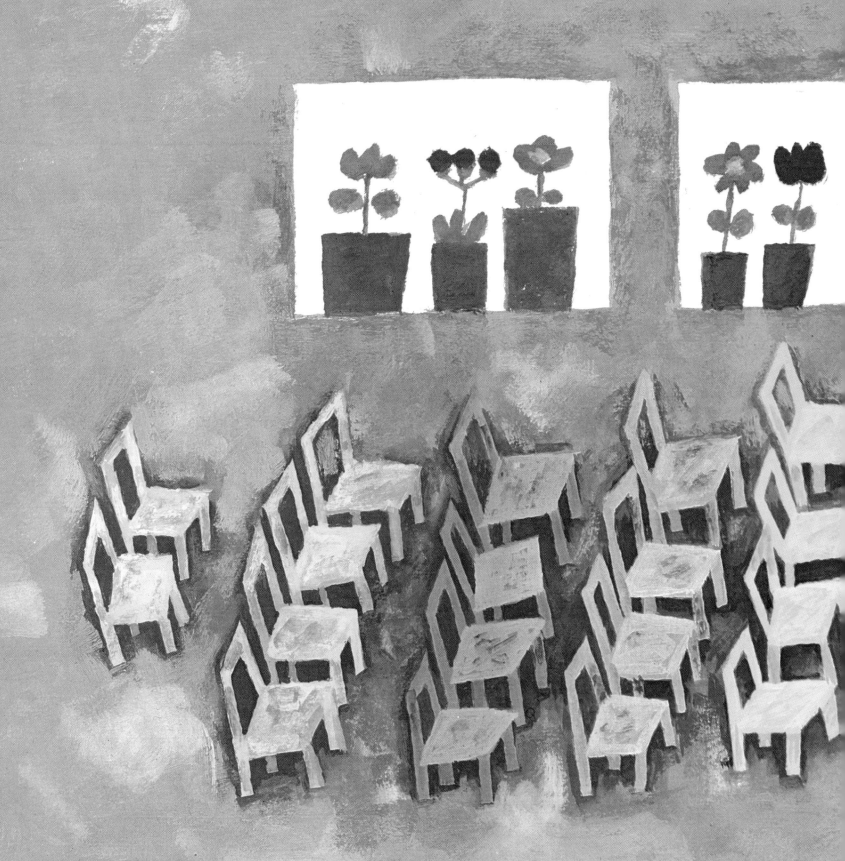

Mr. Bear had come
a long way
and felt very tired.
He put a lot of little chairs
in two rows,
lay down on them
and fell asleep.
But he was too big
for the chairs
and most of them
broke.

He did not know that the house
was a rabbit kindergarten
and he had walked into
one of the classrooms.
When the little rabbits
came back to school after lunch
they could hardly believe
their eyes.

"Who is he?" they said.
"How huge he is."
"Look how many chairs
are broken."

At first the rabbits
were frightened of Mr. Bear,
but when they had had
a good look at him
they did not feel frightened
any more. Some of them began
to make a drawing of him
on the blackboard
and the squeak
of their chalks
woke him up.

He was so upset
about the chairs.
"Towns seem to be
such odd places,"
he said to the teacher.
"Nothing here seems to fit me."

Out in the street again, Mr. Bear found a gang of rabbits
mending the road. It looked easy enough to use a pickaxe

and he thought he would help them.
He did so want to be useful to somebody.

Mr. Bear was good at digging holes.
He lifted the pickaxe high in the air
and brought it down
with all his might—

—straight into
the water main.
Water shot up
all over
everything.
It was like
a fountain.

"Hey, stop that," shouted the rabbit
in charge of the digging.
"What do you think you are doing?"
But Mr. Bear looked so upset
that the rabbit felt sorry for him.
"Cheer up," he said,
"you did your best.
It was kind of you
to try to help."

It was too late; Mr. Bear had decided to go home.
He had brought sacks of presents
for the friends he hoped to make.
He left them all for the rabbits to share.
They watched him trudge away
and waved until he was
out of sight.